# THE CHRISTMAS STICK

## TIM J. MYERS
### Illustrated by NECDET YILMAZ

PARACLETE PRESS

BREWSTER, MASSACHUSETTS

One Christmas Eve in a far kingdom, the royal family gathered to open presents—which mainly meant watching the prince open his.

They were, as usual, magnificent: a mechanical soldier that could sword-fight—a castle with toy knights that moved by themselves—a golden statue of the prince himself—and more.

But the prince never even said thank you. And he was complaining when his grandmother came limping in. She handed him a long, slender box.

Inside he found—a stick. It was sturdy, and as long as he was tall. But it was just a stick.

Before he could say anything, though, his grandmother wished everyone a Merry Christmas and limped from the hall, an odd smile on her face.

That night the prince tossed the stick into a corner and set about playing with his new toys.

The mechanical soldier soon broke, and the royal watchmaker couldn't fix it, so the prince finally threw it off a balcony.

The toy castle was wonderful—but he soon tired of it.

In the same way, his other gifts either fell apart or came to bore him.

One day when he was terribly bored, he noticed the stick. *What good is an old stick?* he fumed. But a few days later his cousin came to visit. She saw the stick and started waving it. "I'm a knight!" she crowed. "Beware my broadsword!"

"Wait!" said the prince. "That's . . . *my* stick!"

After his cousin left, he picked it up. First he pretended it was a sword, killing bandits and dragons with it. Then it was a lance, for jousting.

The next day he needed a flag, so he tied a scarf to the stick and marched under it. Then it became a lute, for playing songs. He started taking it wherever he went.

In the woods it was a shepherd's crook for fighting wolves. Or he'd row with it from a rock in the stream, like a pirate.

It could be a giant's club, a great bow,
a trumpet, a snake to wrestle with.

If he laid it across an open doorway on the battlements, it was strong enough to hang from and swing on.

Soon he was always playing and running about. When friends came they'd all find sticks and be warriors, or wizards with magic staffs—or else hike into the hills with fine walking sticks.

One day he found servants beating some rugs and joined in. Laughing, they pretended they were thrashing terrible ogres. Then the prince noticed the rug before him—the same one his grandmother had limped across last Christmas Eve to give him the stick. That made him think.

When December returned, the kingdom was filled with joy. On Christmas Eve the royal family gathered again.

One by one the gifts were opened. The king and queen found that the prince had given them gifts—which he'd never done before. This brought tears to the queen's eyes; the king sniffed and tried to look stern. When the prince opened his own gifts he said his thanks sincerely each time.

When no gifts were left, everyone rose to leave.

"Wait!" the prince called. Then he brought out one more present and handed it to the queen mother.

When she tore off the paper, she found a stick.

It was sturdy, and as long as she was tall. But the bark had been painstakingly whittled away, the stick then sanded smooth and beautifully varnished. Near the top a leather strip had been tied through a small hole, to make a wristloop. The upper shaft had been wrapped with soft cloth, to ease the holder's grip. And the bottom had a metal tip, to keep it from slipping.

It was just the thing for an old woman with a bad leg, who needed something to lean on. She looked down at the prince— and they smiled knowingly at each other.

And just as she put her arms around him, the bells of Christmas began ringing across the kingdom.

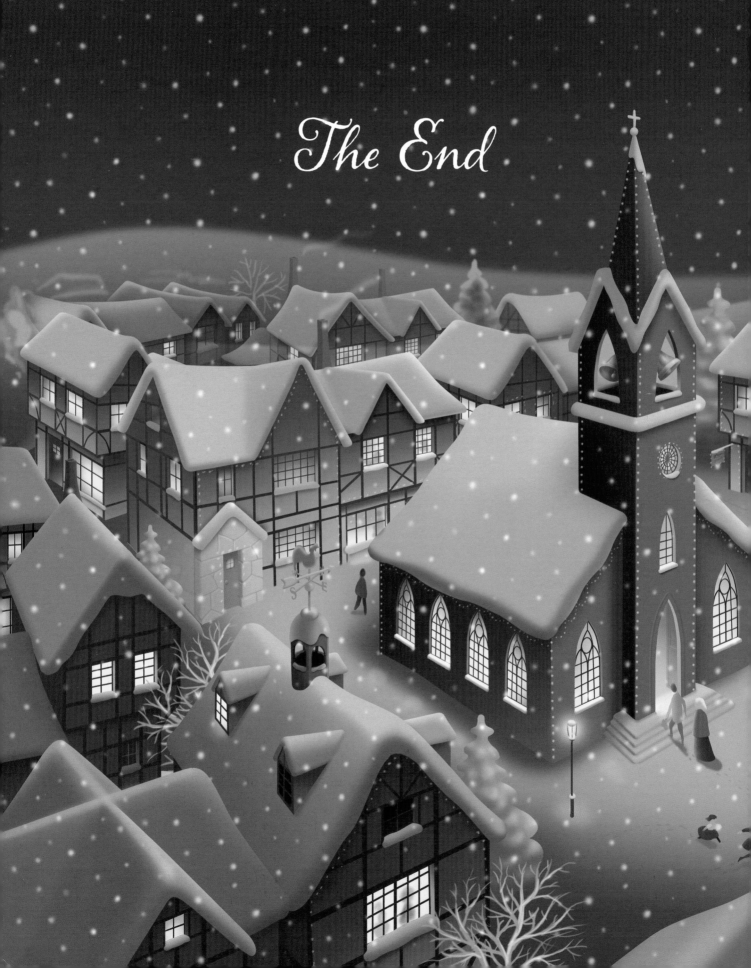

The End

2014 First printing

*The Christmas Stick*

Text copyright © 2014 by Tim J. Myers
Illustrations copyright © 2014 by Necdet Yilmaz

ISBN 978-1-61261-571-4

The Paraclete Press name and logo (dove on cross) are trademarks of Paraclete Press, Inc.

Library of Congress Cataloging-in-Publication Data is available.

10 9 8 7 6 5 4 3 2 1

Published by Paraclete Press
Brewster, Massachusetts
www.paracletepress.com

Printed in the United States of America